This Orchard book

belongs to

....

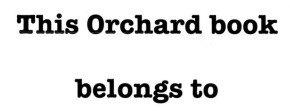

TEN LITTLE MONSTERS

MIKE BROWNLOW SIMON RICKERTY

ORCHARD

Ten little monsters waken from their sleep,

Blinking in the candlelight, in the castle deep.

Going trick or treating, will they frighten you?

Ten little monsters all shout,
"BOO!"

Ten little monsters

hear a chilling whine.

10

. . . nine.

Nine little monsters
run away – but wait!

9

CLANK!

goes the headless knight.

Now there are . . .

...eight.

8

Eight little monsters frightened by a raven.

"CAW!"

flaps the hungry bird.

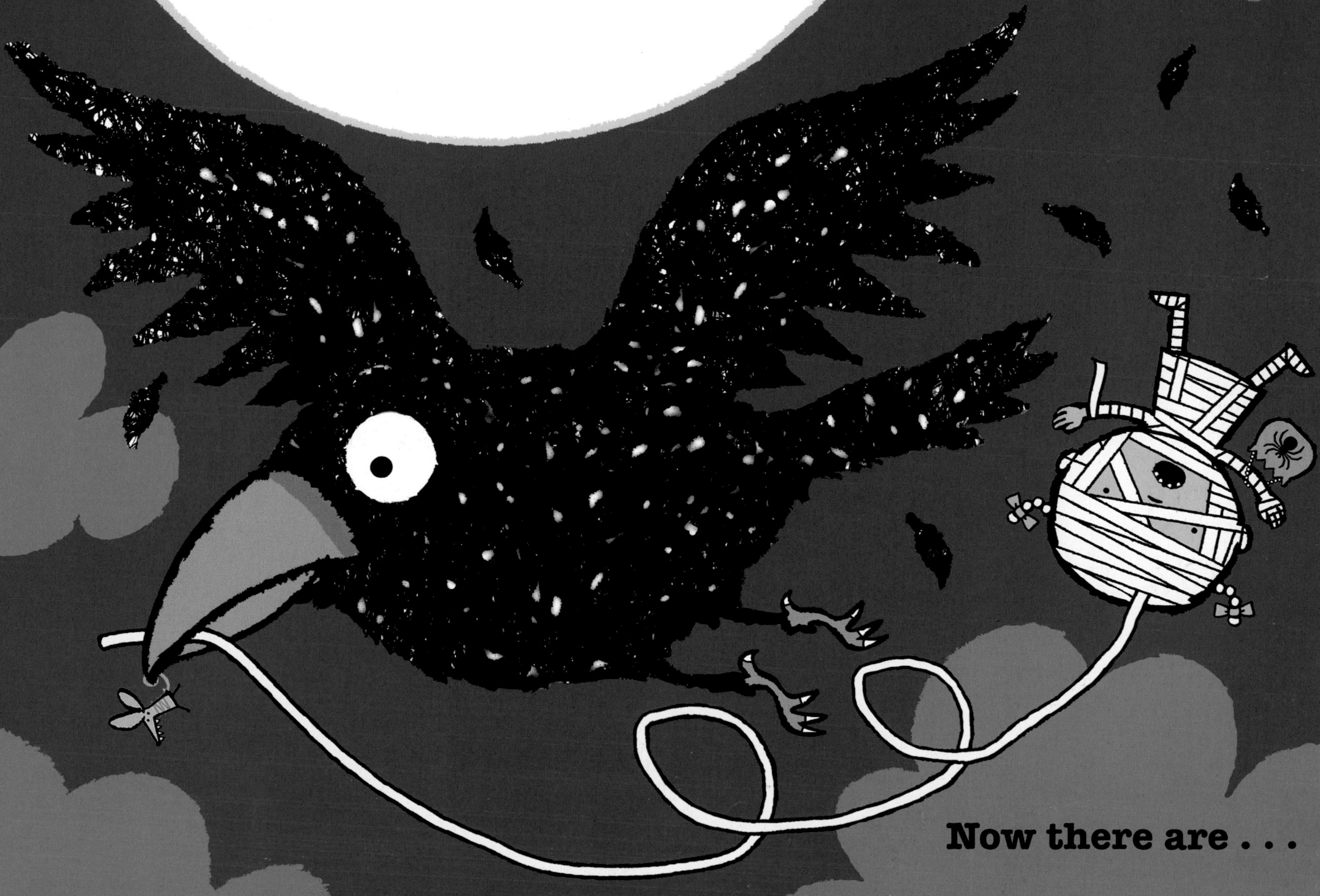

Now there are . . .

Seven little monsters with pumpkin heads on sticks.

7

... **six.**

Six little monsters –
the robot's come alive!

6

"MUAH-HA-HA!"

the scientist laughs.

Now there are . . .

... five.

5

Five little monsters hear scratching at the door.

...four.

Four little monsters, forced to turn and flee.

CLICK

4

CLACK! go the skeletons.

Now there are . . .

. . . three.

Three little monsters smell a stinky brew.

3

"HUBBLE BUBBLE!"

chant the witches.

Now there are . . .

. . . two.

Two little monsters, much too tired to run.

2

"WOO-OOOOOo!"

wails the big, green ghost.

Now there's only . . .

...one.

One little monster, feeling terrified.

1

What's that light?

What's that noise?

Dare he go inside?

"Trick or treat! It's party time!
We wondered where you'd been!"

"Now everyone can celebrate this spooky Halloween!"

Were they very scary?

Did they frighten you?

For Toby. MUAH-HA-HA!
M.B.

For Erin & Isla
S.R.

ORCHARD BOOKS

First published in Great Britain in 2016 by The Watts Publishing Group
This edition first published in 2016

3 5 7 9 10 8 6 4 2

Text © Mike Brownlow, 2016
Illustrations © Simon Rickerty, 2016

A CIP catalogue record for this book is available from the British Library.

ISBN 978 1 40833 403 4

Printed and bound in China

Orchard Books
An imprint of Hachette Children's Group
Part of The Watts Publishing Group Limited
Carmelite House
50 Victoria Embankment
London EC4Y 0DZ

An Hachette UK Company
www.hachette.co.uk

www.hachettechildrens.co.uk